21st Century Junior Library

Plants Need Sunlight

by Jennifer Colby

CHERRY LAKE PUBLISHING * ANN ARBOR, MICHIGAN

Cherry Lake Publishing

Published in the United States of America by Cherry Lake Publishing
Ann Arbor, Michigan
www.cherrylakepublishing.com

Consultants: Elizabeth A. Glynn, Youth Education Coordinator, Matthaei Botanical Gardens and Nichols Arboretum, University of Michigan; Marla Conn, ReadAbility, Inc.

Photo Credits: © Whatafoto/Shutterstock Images, Cover, 16; © Hannamariah/Shutterstock Images, 4; © Casther/Shutterstock Images, 6; © Alena Brozova/Shutterstock Images, 8; © Dorling Kindersley/Thinkstock, 10; © Artens/Shutterstock Images, 12; © Aptyp_koK/Shutterstock Images, 14; © wavebreakmedia/Shutterstock Images, 18; © graham tomlin/Shutterstock Images, 20

LIBRARY OF CONGRESS CATALOGING-IN-PUBLICATION DATA

Colby, Jennifer, 1971-
Plants need sunlight/by Jennifer Colby. - [Revised edition]
pages cm.—(21st century junior library)
Includes bibliographical references and index.
ISBN 978-1-63188-038-4 (hardcover)—ISBN 978-1-63188-124-4 (pdf)—
ISBN 978-1-63188-081-0 (pbk.)—ISBN 978-1-63188-167-1 (ebook)
1. Plants–Effect of light on–Juvenile literature. I. Title. II. Series: 21st century junior library.
QK757.C595 2014
581.7–dc23 2014006226

Cherry Lake Publishing would like to acknowledge the work of The Partnership for 21st Century Skills. Please visit www.p21.org *for more information.*

Printed in the United States of America

CONTENTS

All plants need water, air, sunlight, and nutrients to live and grow.

What Do Plants Eat?

Have you ever wondered what plants eat to live and grow? The answer is plants do not eat at all! Plants make their food. The food plants make gives them energy to live and grow. They only need three **ingredients** to make food. They need water, air, and sunlight. The most important ingredient is sunlight.

Roots take in water and nutrients from the dirt.

Plants also need **nutrients** to stay healthy. Nutrients are not food. They are materials found in dirt and water. Plant roots **absorb** nutrients and water from the dirt.

Look!

Find out why plants need sunlight. Take a photo of two small plants. Put one plant in a sunny window. Put the other plant in a dark closet. Water both plants every day. After one week, take a photo of the plants again. Compare this photo to the first photo you took. How has each plant changed?

Greenhouses use special lamps to help plants grow.

Sunlight is important for plants that grow outside. Some plants grow inside a **greenhouse**. A greenhouse is a building that's just for growing plants.

Greenhouses may use special lamps to give plants extra light. Plants live and grow under these lamps.

Let's take a closer look at how plants use sunlight.

Leaves use water, air, and sunlight to make food.

Making Food

Plants usually make their food in their leaves. Do you remember the three main ingredients plants need to make food? They are water, air, and sunlight. How do these ingredients get to the leaves?

The leaf of a plant absorbs air.

How does a plant absorb water? The roots of a plant are like straws. The roots grow down into the dirt. The roots suck up water from the dirt. Water from the roots flows up the stem through **xylem tissue**. Xylem tissue has tiny tubes that deliver water and nutrients to the leaves.

How does a plant absorb air? The surface of each leaf has many tiny holes in it. These holes are called **stomata**. Air flows into the leaf through these tiny holes.

This is a close-up picture of a leaf. Can you see the tiny green cells of chlorophyll?

How does a plant absorb sunlight? Inside the leaf are tiny green **cells**. These cells have **chlorophyll** in them. The chlorophyll gives the leaf its green color. Its job is to trap light energy.

The leaf uses light energy to combine air and water. This process is called **photosynthesis**. The plant makes a thick liquid sugar. This is the plant's food. This food flows out of the leaves to every part of the plant through **phloem tissue**. Phloem tissue has tiny tubes that deliver food to the plant.

These sunflowers are getting lots of water, air, and sunlight. They will make extra food to store for later.

Energy from the food the plant makes helps the plant grow. The plant uses the food to grow roots, stems, leaves, flowers, fruit, and seeds.

If a plant gets enough water, air, and sunlight, it can make extra food. The extra food is stored inside the roots. The energy from the food can be used later.

Ask Questions!

Some plants need a lot of sunlight to grow. Some plants need just a little. Go to a garden center and ask questions about different plants. Which plants prefer the sun? Which plants prefer the shade?

People get energy from plants.

Sunlight in Your Food

Do you eat carrots? The carrot plant made the carrot by using water, air, and sunlight. You get food energy from the carrot. The energy you get helps you play, think, and grow.

Deer eat plants.

Food energy passes from plants to animals to other animals. This is called the food chain. Some animals eat plants. Some animals eat other animals. Every living thing on Earth is part of the food chain. You are part of the food chain. Almost all food chains begin with water, air, and sunlight.

Make a Guess!

Some animals eat only plants. Some eat only other animals. Some eat plants and animals. Think of an animal. What does it eat? Ask an adult to help you find the answer online or in a book.

GLOSSARY

absorb (ab-ZORB) to take in or soak up

cells (selz) the basic units of all known living things

chlorophyll (KLOR-uh-fil) the green substance in plants that absorbs the light energy needed for a plant to make its own food

greenhouse (GREEN-hous) a building where plants are grown

ingredients (in-GREE-dee-uhnts) things that are used to make something

nutrients (NOO-tree-uhnts) materials found in soil and water that keep plants healthy

phloem tissue (FLOH-em TISH-oo) tubes that carry the plant's food down from the leaves

photosynthesis (foh-toh-SIN-thi-sis) the process of using light energy to combine air and water to make a plant's food

stomata (stoh-MAH-tuh) small holes in the surface of a leaf or stem of a plant that air moves in and out of

xylem tissue (ZAHY-lem TISH-oo) tubes that carry water and nutrients up to a plant's leaves

FIND OUT MORE

BOOKS

Lawrence, Ellen. *Cooking with Sunshine: How Plants Make Food.* New York: Bearport Publishing, 2013.

Stones, Brenda. *What Animals Eat.* New York: Kingfisher, 2012.

WEB SITES

Biology of Plants—Making Food

www.mbgnet.net/bioplants/food.html
A description of photosynthesis and how all food comes from plants.

Education.com—Balloon Greenhouse

www.education.com/activity/article/balloon-greenhouse
Step-by-step instructions on how to make a greenhouse out of a balloon.

INDEX

ABOUT THE AUTHOR

Jennifer Colby is a school librarian, and she also has a bachelor's degree in Landscape Architecture. By writing these books she has combined her talents for two of her favorite things. She likes to garden and grow her own food. In June she makes strawberry jam for her children to enjoy all year long.